TRICK OR TREAT

It was all right for the little children who lived on Willow Street to get all dressed up in strange clothes and put on frightening masks (or paint their faces) on one night each year. And on *that* night they were allowed to go around scaring people and shouting, "Trick or Treat." For that special night was Hallowe'en.

Willow Street was a short street. It was only one block long and the little children were allowed to do their scaring and their shouting *only* on their own block. They would march up to their neighbor's door, ring the bell, and when the door was opened they shouted, "Trick or Treat!"

And since everyone who answered the door always said, "Treat," the children never did any "Tricks." They were always invited in and given some home-made cookies or some candy or apples. Then they would go on to the next house.

But there was one house in the middle of the block where the children never rang the doorbell . . . And they never shouted, "Trick or Treat." That was a very old house with a big rambling hedge in front of it. No one lived there. It was always dark and its big unlit windows looked especially spooky on Hallowe'en. The children called that house the haunted house.

But one Hallowe'en as the Green children, (Lilly and Billy) who were always the first children dressed up and out on the street after supper, were on their way to ring the Browns' doorbell first . . . . they saw something that made them stop short!

Just as they passed the hedge in front of the old haunted house Lilly said:

"Look! . . There're lights!"

Billy turned and looked. And he too saw lights shining through the windows of the old haunted house.

"Let's ring that doorbell first," said Billy, "before we ring the Browns."

"Oh, no," whispered Lilly. "We don't know who lives there."

"Mama said we could ring anybody's doorbell who lives on Willow Street," said Billy. And he walked right up to the front door of the old haunted house and he gave the bell a good pull.

Lilly hurried to join him at the door. She was ready to explain (*if* someone answered the door) that Billy was her little brother . . . and that he may have made a mistake.

They waited for what seemed like a long time.

Then the door creaked and was suddenly opened by a thin little old man with a pointed nose. His white hair, which stood out around his bony head, looked like a sunlit cloud.

"Trick or Treat!" squeaked Billy.

"What? . . . Who?" asked the old man.

Lilly swallowed a lump in her throat and said:

"He said Trick or Treat."

"Oh!" said the little old man, "Trick or Treat? . . . Oh, yes, yes. I say Trick! . . . Come in . . . Come in."

They followed him through the door into the living room.

"Here are two young hobgoblins," said the old man to a little old lady who sat knitting in a rocking chair beside the fireplace. "They came for a Trick."

Lilly and Billy looked at each other. No one had ever said "Trick" before! Everyone always said "Treat" and gave them cookies and apples and other things. They didn't know what to do. They didn't know what to say.

"Sit here," said the little old man, waving his hand to a small sofa. And after Lilly and Billy sat down he said, "Now I shall show you one of my very best Tricks. One moment, please."

He disappeared behind a screen at one end of the room and appeared a moment later with a black cloth and a silver-tipped black wand.

"Now my Trick," he said.

He laid the black cloth flat on a small table. Then he waved his wand over the black cloth and shouted:

"Sassafras Dumplings!"

And he snapped the black cloth quickly up from the table. There stood a large black flowerpot with a pink rosebush growing out of it!

The little old lady put down her knitting and clapped her hands. Lilly and Billy gasped. And before they could think of what to say the doorbell rang.

It was the Brown children, all three of them . . .
Betty, Cathy and Freddie. They were dressed up as
Brownies.

"Trick or Treat!" they shouted together.

"Yes, yes . . . Trick or Treat . . . and I say
Trick," said the little old man. "Come in, come in,
and sit down."

The Brown children walked into the living room. They looked surprised to find Lilly and Billy already sitting there. And after all the Brownies sat down in a bunch in a big armchair, the old man said:

"Now I shall show you another of my very best Tricks."

He waved his wand and the pink rosebush in the black flowerpot lifted itself right up from the table. It sailed over to the little old lady. There the roses and the flowerpot came down gently beside the old lady's chair.

And again the old lady smiled and put down her knitting and clapped her hands together. The old

man stopped her.

"No, no, no! . . . That is not the Trick! Now
here is my Trick."

Once more he covered the table with his black
cloth . . . waved his wand . . . and once more he
picked the black cloth straight up as he shouted,
"Sassafras Dumplings!"

And there on the table standing on end was a broom!

The old man lifted his wand and the broom hopped off the table and swept across the floor until it came to rest against the little old lady's chair.

She clapped her hands good and loud. Then Lilly and Billy clapped their hands and at last all the Brown children timidly clapped their hands too.

The little old man made a deep bow.

"Oh, that was nothing . . . But now I shall . . ."

And before he could finish what he was saying the doorbell rang again.

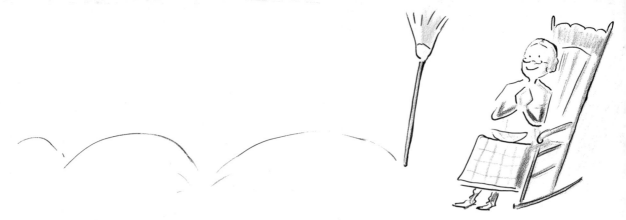

Johnny Grey, dressed up as a cowboy with a big black moustache painted on his face, stood in the open doorway.

"I know . . . I know," said the little old man quickly. "Trick or Treat . . . And I say Trick!"

Johnny Grey's mouth hung open.

"Come in, come in," said the little old man.

Johnny came in and sat down quietly on a stool.

"Now then," said the little old man, "this will be one of my very best Tricks."

And after he covered the little table with the black cloth he waved his silver-tipped wand and shouted, "Sassafras Dumplings" twice! Then he whipped the black cloth straight up from the table.

And there sat a big black cat!

The little old lady clapped her hands together and so did all the children. The big black cat just yawned. Then he blinked and jumped off the table. He walked over to the little old lady and curled up at her feet and went to sleep.

"And now, ladies and gentlemen," said the little old man, "here is my next to my last best Trick."

This time he covered the table with special care. And he fussed with the black cloth until it was exactly right.

"There must be no mistakes to this Trick," he said to the little old lady.

She smiled and nodded brightly. This time the little old man waved his silver-tipped wand over the black cloth in big circles and said, "Sassafras Dumplings! Sassafras Dumplings! Sassafras Dumplings!" . . . real loud.

When he whipped the black cloth off the table there was one of the biggest pumpkin lanterns the children had ever seen! And it was all lit up!

All the children gasped and clapped their hands so loud no one heard the doorbell ring. Whoever it was that rang the bell rang it once more.

"One moment," said the little old man.

He opened the door and in the doorway stood all the other little children who lived on Willow Street. The White twins, Janie and Joanie dressed up like Indians, Benny Black wearing his big sister's hat, shoes, and dress, and Benny's little sister dressed up as a fairy with wings.

"Oh," said the little old man, "more Trick or
Treaters. I'll take Trick. Come in, come in. You are
all welcome."

Janie and Joanie White came in quietly, and Benny
Black, dragging his little sister, stumbled after them
in his big sister's high-heeled shoes.

"I shall do my last and best Trick," said the little
old man.

He picked up the big lit-up pumpkin lantern carefully and set it down in front of the little old lady. Then he switched out all the other lights.

"You all must help me do this Trick," he said. "When I say 'ready,' you all say with me 'Sassafras Dumplings' three times . . . no more and no less. . . . And do say it good and loud."

He spread the black cloth and held it up with both hands like a curtain in front of the little old lady.

"Ready," he said. "Now everybody say good and loud 'Sassafras Dumplings! Sassafras Dumplings! Sassafras Dumplings!' "

All the children shouted with him, "Sassafras Dumplings," three times.

The little old man pulled the black cloth curtain aside. The little old lady had disappeared and sitting in her chair was the nicest little witch anyone had ever seen.

The nice little witch wore a black hat that looked like the black flowerpot that had held the rosebush. The big black cat sat high up on the back of her chair. And she held in one hand the broom and in the other hand a big bunch of pink roses.

The little old man bowed deep and said something that sounded like "Walla."

All the children clapped their hands together. The nice little witch laughed. Of course the children saw right away that the witch was really the little old lady dressed up as a witch.

"This, ladies and gentlemen," said the little old man, "is my last Trick. I would like to introduce myself. I am . . ."

At that moment the doorbell rang once more . . . a long ring.

"Ah . . . This I expect is more children," said

the little old man as he turned toward the front door.

Lilly Green quickly looked around the room.

"No it isn't," she said.

"It isn't?" said the little old man.

"No. All the children who live on Willow Street are here," said Lilly.

Then the doorbell rang again, a long, long ring.

"Well!" said the little old man. "Someone really wants to come in."

He opened the front door wide.

A lot of grownups stuck their heads in the door-way. Since all the lights were out except the lit-up pumpkin, all they could see was the little old man and the nice little witch sitting above the pumpkin lantern. They could not see any of the dressed-up little children seated around the dark room.

"Oh! . . Excuse me," said one of the ladies with her head in the doorway (she sounded like Mrs. Green), "We . . . we are your neighbors . . . Did you see two little children dressed up as hobgoblins?"

"And three little Brownies?" asked another lady.

"Or a cowboy?" said another.

"And two little Indians?" said another.

"And one little fairy with her brother?"

"I should explain," said the first lady who sounded like Mrs. Green. "All our little children have disap-peared . . ."

The little old man clapped his hands together.

"Ah! So you all have come for a Trick," he cried. "Good! This will be my finest Trick . . . Your children have disappeared? So I shall make them appear again!"

He raised his silver-tipped wand with one hand and with the other he put his finger on the light switch on the wall.

"Now," he shouted into the living room, "everyone say 'Sassafras Dumplings'. . . real loud! Ready? . . . Say it!"

"SASSAFRAS DUMPLINGS!" shouted all the little Willow Street children. And at that moment the little man pressed the light switch.

All the children ran laughing and shouting to their mothers.

"Oh! . . . Dear me!" laughed Mrs. Green. "We were all so worried when none of the children came and rang our doorbells. And I had baked so many cookies for the Trick or Treaters. I've been carrying them around looking for children."

Mrs. Green held up the tray she carried. It was full of beautiful cookies with orange icing all over them.

"And I have fudge," said Mrs. Brown, holding up a big plate of maple walnut fudge.

"And I have jelly apples," said Mrs. Grey.

"And I . . . popcorn balls," said Mrs. White.

"And I have chocolate marshmallows," said Mrs. Black.

"We have all been carrying our Treats up and down Willow Street looking for children," said Mrs. Green, "and here they are."

"And I had no Treats for the children," said the little man . . . He sounded sad. "So I did Tricks. Let me introduce myself. I am Professor Purple."

"Oh, a Professor!" said Mrs. Green.

"Yes, I am Professor Purple, the great Magician, retired," said the little man. "And this is my good wife, Mrs. Purple." (He pointed to the nice little witch and she bowed and smiled.) "We just moved into this old house this afternoon while the children were in school. We had no time to get any Hallowe'en Treats . . . That's why I did Tricks for the children. The very same magic Tricks I have done on the stage all over the world . . . even before the crowned heads of Europe . . all three of them."

All the Willow Street grownups smiled and introduced themselves.

Then little Billy Green, who had been a very good boy all evening, pulled his mother's skirt. He wanted to whisper in her ear. And after Mrs. Green listened to Billy she said:

"Oh . . . Mrs. Purple. Billy asked why can't the children have their Hallowe'en Treats right here in your house. We could have a real Hallowe'en party."

Mrs. Purple said that was a very good idea.

So right then and there the Willow Street children had the biggest, the nicest, the best Hallowe'en party they ever had. And they played Hallowe'en games and sang songs until . . .

. . . until it was time to go home . . . through the moonlight . . . and go to bed.

From then on, Professor Purple always did Tricks for the little Willow Street children on Hallowe'en. And all the Willow Street mothers brought their Treats for the children to his house.

Sometimes Professor Purple showed the children how he did his famous magic Tricks. Here on the next page is one Trick that he said he had taught to the crowned heads of Europe . . . all three of them.

You too may be able to do this Trick if you shout "Sassafras Dumplings!" (good and loud).

The Magic Paper Palm Tree Trick

Professor Purple spread out 5 double sheets of old newspaper.
Then he folded them in half.
Then he tore them (one by one) along the fold.
Then he rolled one torn sheet   Then he rolled
another into the first like this   Then another
and another and so on until he had rolled all the torn newspapers into one roll . . . like this
Then he flattened one end of the roll and tore it like this
and he flattened it again and tore it once more.
Now the rolled newspapers looked like this
Then he held the rolled newspaper in one hand and reached into
the top of the roll with the other and he pulled and pulled
and pulled the inside papers straight up until the magic paper
palm tree grew taller than himself.